ANIMALS

Sara Elizabeth Stone

ISBN 978-1-64003-254-5 (Paperback)
ISBN 978-1-64003-255-2 (Digital)

Covenant Books, Inc.
11661 Hwy 707
Murrells Inlet, SC 29576
www.covenantbooks.com

This book is dedicated to four special gifts from God, my grandchildren (Vincent, Nathan, Jordan and Jessica) and to all God's children (of all ages) who love learning about God's creation revealed in nature.

I give special thanks to my husband, Walt, who has given me the freedom and constant support to fulfill God's calling to write about His fingerprint on creation.

Special thanks to my daughter, Christie and long-time friend, Maryann Galt for their love and support that helped make these books a reality.

Also, special thanks to my Mom, who resides in heaven, for teaching me to appreciate how awesome God is as He is revealed through nature, and there is no limit to what we can learn about His creation.

Hello, hello, hello!

It's me again, Moses, the mouse. I hope you read about my first encounter with God, when He showed me how He uses COLORS in this awesome world! He taught me that we should look deeper at the things around us to see His hand in their creation.

You may recall that I live with my mouse family in the basement of a small country church. Mama, Papa, and my sisters are usually inside, but I like to be outside in the fresh air, enjoying the beauty of God's creation.

I often felt lonely. To amuse myself, I would pretend to go on exciting journeys to far-away places. But then one day, God (that's right…God, the creator of the universe), came and spent the day with me, a little mouse, and took me on an adventure I will never forget! He came because of a little prayer that I whispered, asking God to be my friend. Now, I'm not lonely any more. In fact, I find myself talking to Him all the time (now that I know He's always listening). People call it praying, but it's really just having a little heart-to-heart talk with Him any time throughout the day.

Well, it happened again! I was playing outside when I heard God call my name! I got SO excited; my heart started pounding! "Are we going on another adventure?" I asked.

"Yes, my little friend but this one will be very different. Whereas last time I showed you how I use COLOR to make this world more interesting, this time I'm going to show you some animals I created. I can't show you all of them; there are just too many. Moses, I know that you are familiar with the cats, dogs, and rabbits you see running through the church yard, but there is so much more to see. I have animals in every size, shape, and color imaginable, and each has its own unique personality."

"Actually I have so many kinds of animal species that my people can't keep track of them. Every single year they discover a lot of new ones, and some years, thousands of new species! 1) For example, in 2005, they first spotted a pair of nesting Goodman's Mouse Lemurs in Madagascar."

"Mada what?" I asked.

"Madagascar. It's a country very far away from where you live in the United States. Actually, Moses, it's a big world and most of the discoveries of late have been in faraway places. Some of their more recent discoveries include a fanged frog, a "clouded" leopard, and they first spotted what they call a "toothless" rat on an Indonesian island."

I think I heard God chuckle as He said that.

"Actually," God continued, *"that "toothless" rat has fang-like upper teeth which are useless for gnawing and has no back teeth, so it eats only earthworms."*

"That's pretty funny, God. You certainly do make some fascinating creatures, and apparently lots of them!"

"Indeed I do, my little friend. Indeed I do."

I told God I couldn't wait to learn more. Then, it happened again. Suddenly, I was very sleepy and had to lie down and close my eyes.

Then, we were instantly somewhere I'd never been. I'm still not sure where it was exactly, but it was very hot and I was looking at some huge, dusty animals.

"Moses, these are camels that you're looking at and we're in the desert, where it's sandy and hot."

"You're right about that!" I told God. "It certainly is hot!"

"Well, the heat and sand can be pretty hard on people, especially during sand storms, so I made camels to help them get around. This one is a dromedary camel, it has one hump on its back and is built to withstand the heat. But I also made the Bactrian camel, which has two humps, longer fur, and can withstand extreme heat or cold. People ride on camels and hang heavy loads on them for traveling long distances in the desert.

My people think the humps are filled with water, but they aren't. They're filled with fat, which allows the camel to go long periods without food or water. Camels have two 2) bushy eyebrows that protect them from the sun, a double row of long eyelashes, and clear inner eyelids, which protect their eyes from sandstorms while still letting in enough light for the camels to see. They also have hairs in their ears to help stop blowing sand from filling up their ears and they can even close their nostrils when necessary."

"Wow, God, you really put a lot of thought and care into Your creations. I don't have the words to describe it all. It's so wonderful, so unique, so awesome . . . so terrific that I think I need a new word to describe everything. Awesome-erific. Yes, that's it . . . that's my new word!"

"Awesome what?" God laughed and said, *"I like that Moses! I think you're pretty awesome-erific too!"*

"While I'm showing you how the animals have built-in defenses, like the eye lids and lashes on the camel, let me tell you about some other animals and the unique ways they defend themselves. For example, there's the skunk, which sprays oil when it feels threatened. It's very strong and the smell is hard to get rid of. People learn quickly that it's a good thing to stay away from the back end of a skunk!

Then, there's the possum and opossum (over 170 species between the two, which are similar, but not the same)."

"There you go again, God. Couldn't you just make two or three or ten or twenty types? How could you possibly come up with that many types?"

"Anyway, Moses, the possum and opossum have a funny way of protecting themselves. They play dead."

"Seriously?" I asked.

"Yes, they become limp, drool, and even smell dead. In fact, my people call it 'playing possum' when they're pretending to be asleep."

I told God, "That seems impossible. Only a big God like you could create such awesome-erific animals!"

"Well, my little friend, I was showing you how some of my animal kingdom protect themselves. Some have antlers, some have horns, and some have tusks that they can use for lots of things including self-defense. I gave antlers to the caribou, deer, and moose. 3) In fact, the antlers on a moose can catch sound waves like a giant hearing aid so they can hear each other's calls from up to two miles away."

"That's amazing, God" I said.

"And my reindeer use their antlers to clear the snow to find food. Unlike horns, 4) antlers are shed and regrown each year. 5) Horns, however, are different than antlers, which can be found on bulls, goats, rhinoceros [rhinos], rams, buffalo, antelope, and even some lizards. Generally, they keep their horns throughout their lifetime."

"Now I'll tell you about tusks. Two of the heaviest animals on earth are the elephant and hippopotamus (hippo), and they both have tusks (made of ivory) though the elephant tusks are much longer like that of the walrus. It's interesting to know that tusks are actually teeth that grew very long."

I told God "I hope my teeth don't grow that long."

"Oh Moses, you're so funny; don't worry, that won't happen. As I was saying, 6) Elephants also have long trunks with over one hundred thousand muscle fibers, which are used for breathing, smelling, touching, picking things up, and making sounds. Their sense of smell can be up to four times as sensitive as that of a bloodhound (a dog known for its good sense of smell). Elephants can suck up water to drink and spray on their bodies. When underwater, the elephant can use its trunk as a snorkel."

"What an awesome-erific invention, that trunk thing is!" I exclaimed.

"My people say elephants have good memories and they're right. 7) When it comes to smarts, elephants are right up there with dolphins, apes, and people."

I told God how I love hearing about all these things and how much I was enjoying our adventure!

Now you see me

Now you don't

"*Moses, do you remember I taught you about camouflage on our first adventure?*" God asked.

"Oh, yes, I think I do! That's how You gave some of Your creatures different colors or textures to hide and protect themselves."

"*Good memory, little mouse. You are correct. Now I'll show you some more ways animals defend themselves. 8)The armadillo, for example, has an armor plating outside that covers the back, head, legs, and tail of these odd-looking creatures. Of the twenty species of armadillo that range from as little as six inches up to five feet in length—ten times as big—one specie can even tuck its head and back feet inside to become a hard ball, fully encased. It's similar to my turtles, tortoises, and terrapins.*

"*9) They are all reptiles and have shells, but the basic difference between them is turtles live in water for the most part, tortoises live on land, and terrapins are a bit of both. Tortoises, which can grow to be quite large, can completely retract their heads into their shells where most turtles can't and terrapins fold theirs sideways.*

"Then there's the interesting little porcupine. 10) Some have up to thirty thousand sharp arrow-like spears called quills. People think that the porcupine can aim and shoot the quills, but they really can't. The quills are like needles with sharp tips and barbs on the ends. Their design allows them to pierce a predator's skin easily even at the slightest touch, but the barbs on the ends make the quills difficult and painful to remove.

North American porcupines love to eat wood, including tree bark, as well as fruit and leaves. Being good climbers, they spend a lot of time in trees, and being a larger animal, they tend to fall out of trees quite often. And then, guess what happens. The porcupine sticks itself with its own quills! So, to protect the porcupines from getting infections, I put a greasy coating on each quill that contains an antibiotic, which is medicine."

"What an awesome God you are! You really are awesome-erific!"

"I want to show you the color patterns on some of my animals. The black and white striped animals you see are zebras", God said. "Each one is different. 11) No two zebras have the same pattern of stripes."

"Seriously, each one is different?" I asked.

"Yes, and look at the tiger, which is much more colorful with shades of orange, yellow, or white with the black or brown stripes, yet each animal is unique; no two have the same stripes. 11) And it is interesting to note that you'd find a black skin under the zebra's hair, and if you shave a tiger, you'll find the same pattern on his skin that's shown on his fur."

"Then look over there. You'll see a sleeping leopard. No stripes. Instead, it has spots!

In the distance, you'll see a couple of giraffes. Those are the ones with the long legs and necks. Again, 12) no two have the same pattern of spots! And my giraffes are the tallest animals in the world! Their long legs are often as tall as a grown man, which allows them to run very fast. Giraffes are known for the very long necks that can reach high into the trees to eat the leaves. And even their tongues are long to help them get those leaves off the trees. But it is difficult for the giraffe to spread its long legs and bend down to drink. So I made them in such a way that they don't have to drink as often as other animals; they only need to drink every few days. They get most of their water from the luscious plants they eat."

"You never cease to amaze me," I said. "You are . . . well, You know."

"Awesome-erific?" asked God as He chuckled.

"Moses, you know those cats, dogs, and rabbits you see running through the church yard?"

I told God that I do, but I hide so quickly when they're around and I've really only had a glimpse of them.

"Well, Moses, cats, dogs, and rabbits—and other animals, like foxes, ferrets, and even big cats like lions and tigers—all have whiskers. They are hairs that are thicker and longer than the fur and help them in different ways. Most people don't know it but they really do serve a purpose; they're not just decoration. Whiskers are sensitive to the touch and sensitive to vibration which helps them know what's around them. And the whiskers on cats and rabbits are generally the same width as their bodies which allows them to know if they will fit into a small space."

"Oh, God, what detail went into Your creations! You've thought of everything!"

"Some other animals you may have spotted from the church yard are animals on the farm next to the church," God said, as He placed me atop the white picket fence where I could see all the farm animals!

I told God I had never seen any of the animals, but I certainly have heard them. In fact, I hear all kinds of sounds from over there. God said He's given interesting sounds to many of the animals including farm animals. For example:

birds chirp, coo and caw   chickens cluck
dogs bark   elephants trumpet
pigs oink   sheep bah
cats both meow and purr   cows moo
ducks quack   horses neigh
roosters crow   turkeys gobble

"This farm has chickens, cows and pigs. The girl chickens are hens and lay eggs, and the boys are roosters, which crow first thing every morning. The cows give milk. So not only do the animals make different sounds, they serve different purposes and are useful to my people in lots of different ways! On some other farms, you might find sheep, donkeys, horses, ducks, or goats."

"Thanks, God, for showing me the farm. It's nice to see where all those sounds come from, especially those noisy roosters!"

"Well, Moses, that's enough for today," God said to me.

And I was instantly back under the flowers where I hide. I felt I was waking up from a nap, but I knew God had just taken me on another fabulous journey!

"Oh, God, thank you, thank you, thank you! And thanks again for being my friend...my very best friend! You are such a wonderful God!"

I knew my adventure was over for today, and I couldn't wait to go home and tell Mama, Papa, and my sisters about all God showed me! As a family, we are starting to realize why the people in this church seem so happy when they sing about God or sing praises to Him. He cares about everyone, everything, and about every little detail. He is so loving, caring, and...well...awesome-erific!

As I poked my head through the flowers where I was hiding so I could hurry home, I saw a rainbow. It was breathtaking, just like the one I'd seen before, but this time I knew for certain that it was just for me!

Don't forget, next time you see a rainbow, ask yourself if maybe God made that just for you! And by the way, He loves it when you talk to Him! You can talk to Him about anything! He'd love hearing from you! He's always watching over you and listening for your voice!

And when you're outside, stop a minute, look around, and take the time to appreciate the wonders of His creation.

Till next time.

REFERENCES

The information in this book is not intended to be all inclusive, but to give the reader a nugget of information on each subject, making them hungry to do more library and/or on-line searches for themselves. There is so much more information about each subject, it is my hope that the reader will use the reference sites only as a jumping off point.

Page 5:

1. http://www.theguardian.com/environment/gallery/2014/may/22/top-10-new-species-of-the-past-year-in-pictures Scroll to see (and click on) "Meet the top 10 newly discovered species of 2014" (from 18,000 newly identified)

Page 8:

2. https://kidskonnect.com/animals/camel

Page 11:

3. http://news.bbc.co.uk/cbbcnews/hi/newsid_7300000/newsid_7308400/7308470.stm

4. https://en.wikipedia.org/wiki/Antler

Page 12:

5. http://www.nps.gov/yell/learn/kidsyouth/ahdiff.htm

Page 14

6. https://en.wikipedia.org/wiki/Elephant#trunk
7. http://www.scientificamerican.com/article/elephants-never-forget

Page 16

8. http://animals.nationalgeographic.com/animals/mammals/armadillo
9. http://www.londolozi.com/cubsden/whats-the-difference-between-turtles-tortoises-and-terrapins

Page 18

10. http://wonderopolis.org/wonder/can-porcupines-shoot-their-quills/

Page 19

11. http://animals.mom.me/difference-between-zebra-tiger-stripes-7930.html

Page 22

12. http://animals.nationalgeographic.com/animals/mammals/giraffe/

ABOUT THE AUTHOR

Sara Elizabeth Stone

Sara is a Christian whose love of nature started as a little girl in Bucks County, Pennsylvania. Her Mom loved nature, and spent a lot of time in the garden. She would show Sara how the tiniest of bugs (so tiny you can hardly see it) has a heart, stomach, brain, eyes, etc. That began Sara's life-long appreciation for all the "little miracles" in God's creation that are often overlooked or under-appreciated. Sara now lives in Carroll County, Maryland with her husband, near her daughter and son-in-law, and spends much of her time with her grandchildren.

Even though Sara loves spending time with God as he orchestrates the writing of the Creation Series, Sara discovered there is a deeper thread running through the books that reveals the heart of God, as He seeks relationship with his children (at every age).

CPSIA information can be obtained
at www.ICGtesting.com
Printed in the USA
BVHW02s0151130418
513054BV00006B/13/P